ALAN LIGHTMAN

EINSTEIN'S DREAMS

Alan Lightman was born in Memphis, Tennessee, in 1948 and educated at Princeton and at the California Institute of Technology, where he received a Ph.D. in theoretical physics. His research papers in physics have appeared in numerous scientific journals. His essays and reviews have appeared in *The Atlantic*, *Harper's*, *The New Yorker*, *Nature*, *The New York Review of Books*, and other publications. His books include several books on science, two collections of essays, a book of poetry, and five novels. His *Einstein's Dreams* was an international bestseller, and *The Diagnosis* was a finalist for the National Book Award in fiction. Lightman has served on the faculties of Harvard University and the Massachusetts Institute of Technology, where he was one of the first people to receive a joint appointment in science and in the humanities. Lightman is also the founding director of the Harpswell Foundation, a non-profit that works to empower women in Cambodia.

BOOKS BY ALAN LIGHTMAN

Science

Origins

Ancient Light

Great Ideas in Physics

The Discoveries

Essays

Dance for Two

A Sense of the Mysterious

Fiction

Einstein's Dreams

Good Benito

The Diagnosis

Reunion

Ghost

Poetry

Song of Two Worlds

EINSTEIN'S DREAMS

ALAN LIGHTMAN

VINTAGE CONTEMPORARIES

Vintage Books

A Division of Random House, Inc.

New York

FIRST VINTAGE CONTEMPORARIES EDITION, NOVEMBER 2004

Copyright © 1993 by Alan Lightman
Illustrations copyright © 1993 by Chris Costello

All rights reserved under International and Pan-American Copyright Conventions. Published in the United States by Vintage Books, a division of Random House, Inc., New York, and simultaneously in Canada by Random House of Canada Limited, Toronto. Originally published in hardcover in the United States by Pantheon Books, a division of Random House, Inc., New York, in 1993.

Vintage and colophon are registered trademarks and Vintage Contemporaries is a trademark of Random House, Inc.

The Library of Congress has cataloged the Pantheon edition as follows:
Lightman, Alan P., 1948–
Einstein's dreams / Alan Lightman.
p. cm.
1. Einstein, Albert. 1879–1955—Fiction.   I. Title.
PS3562.I45397E38 1993
813'.54—dc20
92-50465

Vintage ISBN: 1-4000-7780-X

www.vintagebooks.com

Printed in the United States of America
20

EINSTEIN'S DREAMS

In some distant arcade, a clock tower calls out six times and then stops. The young man slumps at his desk. He has come to the office at dawn, after another upheaval. His hair is uncombed and his trousers are too big. In his hand he holds twenty crumpled pages, his new theory of time, which he will mail today to the German journal of physics.

Tiny sounds from the city drift through the room. A milk bottle clinks on a stone. An awning is cranked in a shop on Marktgasse. A vegetable cart moves slowly through a street. A man and woman talk in hushed tones in an apartment nearby.

In the dim light that seeps through the room, the desks appear shadowy and soft, like large sleeping animals. Except for the young man's desk, which is cluttered with half-opened books, the twelve oak desks are all neatly covered with documents, left from the previous day. Upon arriving in two hours, each clerk will know precisely where to begin. But at this moment, in this dim light, the documents on the desks are no more visible than the clock in the corner or the secretary's stool near the door. All that can be seen at this moment are the shadowy shapes of the desks and the hunched form of the young man.

Ten minutes past six, by the invisible clock on the wall. Minute by minute, new objects gain form. Here, a brass wastebasket appears. There, a calendar on a wall. Here, a family photograph, a box of paper clips, an inkwell, a pen. There, a typewriter, a jacket folded on a chair. In time, the ubiquitous bookshelves emerge from the night mist that hangs on the walls. The bookshelves hold notebooks of patents. One patent concerns a new drilling gear with teeth curved in a pattern to minimize friction. Another proposes an electrical transformer that holds constant voltage when the power supply varies. Another describes a typewriter with a low-velocity typebar that eliminates noise. It is a room full of practical ideas.

Outside, the tops of the Alps start to glow from the sun. It is late June. A boatman on the Aare unties his small skiff and pushes off, letting the current take him along Aarstrasse to Gerberngasse, where he will deliver his summer apples and berries. The baker arrives at his store on Marktgasse, fires his coal oven, begins mixing flour and yeast. Two lovers embrace on the Nydegg Bridge, gaze wistfully into the river below. A man stands on his balcony on Schifflaube, studies the pink sky. A woman who cannot sleep walks slowly down Kramgasse, peering into each dark arcade, reading the posters in half-light.

In the long, narrow office on Speichergasse, the room full of practical ideas, the young patent clerk still sprawls in his chair, head down on his desk. For the past several months, since the middle of April, he has dreamed many dreams about time. His dreams have taken hold of his research. His dreams have worn him out, exhausted him so that he sometimes cannot tell whether he is awake or asleep. But the dreaming is finished. Out of many possible natures of time, imagined in as many nights, one seems compelling. Not that the others are impossible. The others might exist in other worlds.

The young man shifts in his chair, waiting for the typist to come, and softly hums from Beethoven's *Moonlight* Sonata.

• 14 APRIL 1905

Suppose time is a circle, bending back on itself. The world repeats itself, precisely, endlessly.

For the most part, people do not know they will live their lives over. Traders do not know that they will make the same bargain again and again. Politicians do not know that they will shout from the same lectern an infinite number of times in the cycles of time. Parents treasure the first laugh from their child as if they will not hear it again. Lovers making love the first time undress shyly, show surprise at the supple thigh, the fragile nipple. How would they know that each secret glimpse, each touch, will be repeated again and again and again, exactly as before?

On Marktgasse, it is the same. How could the shopkeepers know that each handmade sweater, each embroidered handkerchief, each chocolate candy, each intricate compass and watch will return to their stalls? At dusk, the shopkeepers go home to their families or drink beer in the taverns, calling happily to friends down the vaulted alleys, caressing each moment as an emerald on temporary consignment. How could they know that nothing is temporary, that all will happen again? No more than an ant crawling round the rim of a crystal chandelier knows that it will return to where it began.

In the hospital on Gerberngasse, a woman says goodbye to her husband. He lies in bed and stares at her emptily. In the last two months, his cancer has spread from his throat to his liver, his pancreas, his brain. His two young children sit on one chair in the corner of the room, frightened to look at their father, his sunken cheeks, the withered skin of an old man. The wife comes to the bed and kisses her husband softly on the forehead, whispers goodbye, and quickly leaves with the children. She is certain that this was the last kiss. How could she know that time will begin again, that she will be born again, will study at the gymnasium again, will show her paintings at the gallery in Zürich, will again meet her husband in the small library in Fribourg, will again go sailing with him in Thun Lake on a warm day in July, will give birth again, that her husband will again work for eight years at the pharmaceutical and come home one evening with a lump in his throat, will again throw up and get weak and end up in this hospital, this room, this bed, this moment. How could she know?

In the world in which time is a circle, every handshake, every kiss, every birth, every word, will be repeated precisely. So too every moment that two friends stop becoming friends, every time that a family is broken because of money, every vicious remark in an argument between spouses, every opportunity denied because of a superior's jealousy, every promise not kept.

And just as all things will be repeated in the future, all things now happening happened a million times before. Some few people in every town, in their dreams, are vaguely aware that all has occurred in the past. These are the people with unhappy lives, and they sense that their misjudgments and wrong deeds and bad luck have all taken place in the previous loop of time. In the dead of night these cursed citizens wrestle with their bedsheets, unable to rest, stricken with the knowledge that they cannot change a single action, a single gesture. Their mistakes will be repeated precisely in this life as in the life before. And it is these double unfortunates who give the only sign that time is a circle. For in each town, late at night, the vacant streets and balconies fill up with their moans.

In this world, time is like a flow of water, occasionally displaced by a bit of debris, a passing breeze. Now and then, some cosmic disturbance will cause a rivulet of time to turn away from the mainstream, to make connection backstream. When this happens, birds, soil, people caught in the branching tributary find themselves suddenly carried to the past.

Persons who have been transported back in time are easy to identify. They wear dark, indistinct clothing and walk on their toes, trying not to make a single sound, trying not to bend a single blade of grass. For they fear that any change they make in the past could have drastic consequences for the future.

Just now, for example, such a person is crouching in the shadows of the arcade, at no. 19 Kramgasse. An odd place for a traveler from the future, but there she is. Pedestrians pass, stare, and walk on. She huddles in a corner, then quickly creeps across the street and cowers in another darkened spot, at no. 22. She is terrified that she will kick up dust, just as a Peter Klausen is making his way to the apothecary on Spital-gasse this afternoon of 16 April 1905. Klausen is something of a dandy and hates to have his clothes sullied. If dust messes his clothes, he will stop and painstakingly brush them off, regardless of waiting appointments. If Klausen is sufficiently delayed, he may not buy the ointment for his wife, who has been complaining of leg aches for weeks. In that case, Klausen's wife, in a bad humor, may decide not to make the trip to Lake Geneva. And if she does not go to Lake Geneva on 23 June 1905, she will not meet a Catherine d'Épinay walking on the jetty of the east shore and will not introduce Mlle. d'Épinay to her son Richard. In turn, Richard and Catherine will not marry on 17 December 1908, will not give birth to Friedrich on 8 July 1912. Friedrich Klausen will not be father to Hans

Klausen on 22 August 1938, and without Hans Klausen the European Union of 1979 will never occur.

The woman from the future, thrust without warning into this time and this place and now attempting to be invisible in her darkened spot at no. 22 Kramgasse, knows the Klausen story and a thousand other stories waiting to unfold, dependent on the births of children, the movement of people in the streets, the songs of birds at certain moments, the precise position of chairs, the wind. She crouches in the shadows and does not return the stares of people. She crouches and waits for the stream of time to carry her back to her own time.

When a traveler from the future must talk, he does not talk but whimpers. He whispers tortured sounds. He is agonized. For if he makes the slightest alteration in anything, he may destroy the future. At the same time, he is forced to witness events without being part of them, without changing them. He envies the people who live in their own time, who can act at will, oblivious of the future, ignorant of the effects of their actions. But he cannot act. He is an inert gas, a ghost, a sheet without soul. He has lost his personhood. He is an exile of time.

Such wretched people from the future can be found in every

village and every town, hiding under the eaves of buildings, in basements, under bridges, in deserted fields. They are not questioned about coming events, about future marriages, births, finances, inventions, profits to be made. Instead, they are left alone and pitied.

It is a cold morning in November and the first snow has fallen. A man in a long leather coat stands on his fourth-floor balcony on Kramgasse overlooking the Zähringer Fountain and the white street below. To the east, he can see the fragile steeple of St. Vincent's Cathedral, to the west, the curved roof of the Zytgloggeturm. But the man is not looking east or west. He is staring down at a tiny red hat left in the snow below, and he is thinking. Should he go to the woman's house in Fribourg? His hands grip the metal balustrade, let go, grip again. Should he visit her? Should he visit her?

He decides not to see her again. She is manipulative and judgmental, and she could make his life miserable. Perhaps she would not be interested in him anyway. So he decides not to see her again. Instead, he keeps to the company of men. He works hard at the pharmaceutical, where he hardly notices the female assistant manager. He goes to the brasserie on Kocher-gasse in the evenings with his friends and drinks beer, he learns to make fondue. Then, in three years, he meets another woman in a clothing shop in Neuchâtel. She is nice. She makes love to him very very slowly, over a period of months. After a year, she comes to live with him in Berne. They live quietly, take walks together along the Aare, are companions to each other, grow old and contented.

In the second world, the man in the long leather coat decides that he must see the Fribourg woman again. He hardly knows her, she could be manipulative, and her movements hint at volatility, but that way her face softens when she smiles, that laugh, that clever use of words. Yes, he must see her again. He goes to her house in Fribourg, sits on the couch with her, within moments feels his heart pounding, grows weak at the sight of the white of her arms. They make love, loudly and with pas-sion. She persuades him to move to Fribourg. He leaves his job in Berne and begins work at the Fribourg Post Bureau. He burns with his love for her. Every day he comes home at noon. They eat, they make love, they argue, she complains that she needs more money, he pleads with her, she throws pots at him, they make love again, he returns to the Post Bureau. She threatens to leave him, but she does not leave him. He lives for her, and he is happy with his anguish.

In the third world, he also decides that he must see her again. He hardly knows her, she could be manipulative, and her movements hint at volatility, but that smile, that laugh, that clever use of words. Yes, he must see her again. He goes to her house in Fribourg, meets her at the door, has tea with her at her kitchen table. They talk of her work at the library, his job at the pharmaceutical. After an hour, she says that she must leave to help a friend, she says goodbye to him, they shake hands. He travels the thirty kilometers back to Berne, feels empty during the train ride home, goes to his fourth-floor apartment on Kramgasse, stands on the balcony and stares down at the tiny red hat left in the snow.

These three chains of events all indeed happen, simultaneously. For in this world, time has three dimensions, like space. Just as an object may move in three perpendicular directions, corresponding to horizontal, vertical, and longitudinal, so an object may participate in three perpendicular futures. Each future moves in a different direction of time. Each future is real. At every point of decision, whether to visit a woman in Fribourg or to buy a new coat, the world splits into three worlds, each with the same people but with different fates for those people. In time, there are an infinity of worlds.

Some make light of decisions, arguing that all possible decisions will occur. In such a world, how could one be responsible for his actions? Others hold that each decision must be considered and committed to, that without commitment there is chaos. Such people are content to live in contradictory worlds, so long as they know the reason for each.

• 24 APRIL 1905

In this world, there are two times. There is mechanical time and there is body time. The first is as rigid and metallic as a massive pendulum of iron that swings back and forth, back and forth, back and forth. The second squirms and wriggles like a bluefish in a bay. The first is unyielding, predetermined. The second makes up its mind as it goes along.

Many are convinced that mechanical time does not exist. When they pass the giant clock on the Kramgasse they do not see it; nor do they hear its chimes while sending packages on

Postgasse or strolling between flowers in the Rosengarten. They wear watches on their wrists, but only as ornaments or as courtesies to those who would give timepieces as gifts. They do not keep clocks in their houses. Instead, they listen to their heartbeats. They feel the rhythms of their moods and desires. Such people eat when they are hungry, go to their jobs at the millinery or the chemist's whenever they wake from their sleep, make love all hours of the day. Such people laugh at the thought of mechanical time. They know that time moves in fits and starts. They know that time struggles forward with a weight on its back when they are rushing an injured child to the hospital or bearing the gaze of a neighbor wronged. And they know too that time darts across the field of vision when they are eating well with friends or receiving praise or lying in the arms of a secret lover.

Then there are those who think their bodies don't exist. They live by mechanical time. They rise at seven o'clock in the morning. They eat their lunch at noon and their supper at six. They arrive at their appointments on time, precisely by the clock. They make love between eight and ten at night. They work forty hours a week, read the Sunday paper on Sunday, play chess on Tuesday nights. When their stomach growls, they look at their watch to see if it is time to eat. When they begin to lose themselves in a concert, they look at the clock above the stage to see when it will be time to go home. They know that the body is not a thing of wild magic, but a collection of chemicals, tissues, and nerve impulses. Thoughts are no more than electrical surges in the brain. Sexual arousal is no more than a flow of chemicals to certain nerve endings. Sadness no more than a bit of acid transfixed in the cerebellum. In short, the body is a machine, subject to the same laws of electricity and mechanics as an electron or clock. As such, the body must be addressed in the language of physics. And if the body speaks, it is the speaking only of so many levers and forces. The body is a thing to be ordered, not obeyed.

Taking the night air along the river Aare, one sees evidence for two worlds in one. A boatman gauges his position in the dark by counting seconds drifted in the water's current. "One, three meters. Two, six meters. Three, nine meters." His voice cuts through the black in clean and certain syllables. Beneath a lamppost on the Nydegg Bridge, two brothers who have not seen each other for a year stand and drink and laugh. The bell of St. Vincent's Cathedral sings ten times. In seconds, lights in the apartments lining Schifflaube wink out, in a perfect mechanized response, like the deductions of Euclid's geometry. Lying on the riverbank, two lovers look up lazily, awakened from a timeless sleep by the distant church bells, surprised to find that night has come.

Where the two times meet, desperation. Where the two times go their separate ways, contentment. For, miraculously, a barrister, a nurse, a baker can make a world in either time, but not in both times. Each time is true, but the truths are not the same.

In this world, it is instantly obvious that something is odd. No houses can be seen in the valleys or plains. Everyone lives in the mountains.

At some time in the past, scientists discovered that time flows more slowly the farther from the center of earth. The effect is minuscule, but it can be measured with extremely sensitive instruments. Once the phenomenon was known, a few people, anxious to stay young, moved to the mountains. Now all houses are built on Dom, the Matterhorn, Monte Rosa, and other high ground. It is impossible to sell living quarters elsewhere.

Many are not content simply to locate their homes on a mountain. To get the maximum effect, they have constructed their houses on stilts. The mountaintops all over the world are nested with such houses, which from a distance look like a flock of fat birds squatting on long skinny legs. People most eager to live longest have built their houses on the highest stilts. Indeed, some houses rise half a mile high on their spindly wooden legs. Height has become status. When a person from his kitchen window must look up to see a neighbor, he believes that neighbor will not become stiff in the joints as soon as he, will not lose his hair until later, will not wrinkle until later, will not lose the urge for romance as early. Likewise, a person looking down on another house tends to dismiss its occupants as spent, weak, and shortsighted. Some boast that they have lived their whole lives high up, that they were born in the highest house on the highest mountain peak and have never descended. They celebrate their youth in their mirrors and walk naked on their balconies.

Now and then some urgent business forces people to come down from their houses, and they do so with haste, hurrying down their tall ladders to the ground, running to another ladder or to the valley below, completing their transactions, and then returning as quickly as possible to their houses, or to other high places. They know that with each downward step, time passes just a little bit faster and they age a little more quickly. People at ground level never sit. They run, while carrying their briefcases or groceries.

A small number of residents in each city have stopped caring whether they age a few seconds faster than their neighbors. These adventuresome souls come down to the lower world for days at a time, lounge under the trees that grow in the valleys, swim leisurely in the lakes that lie at warmer altitudes, roll on level ground. They hardly look at their watches and cannot tell you if it is Monday or Thursday. When the others rush by them and scoff, they just smile.

In time, people have forgotten the reason why higher is better. Nonetheless, they continue to live on the mountains, to avoid sunken regions as much as they can, to teach their children to shun other children from low elevations. They tolerate the cold of the mountains by habit and enjoy the discomfort as part of their breeding. They have even convinced themselves that thin air is good for their bodies and, following that logic, have gone on spare diets, refusing all but the most gossamer food. At length, the populace have become thin like the air, bony, old before their time.

One cannot walk down an avenue, converse with a friend, enter a building, browse beneath the sandstone arches of an old arcade without meeting an instrument of time. Time is visible in all places. Clock towers, wristwatches, church bells divide years into months, months into days, days into hours, hours into seconds, each increment of time marching after the other in perfect succession. And beyond any particular clock, a vast scaffold of time, stretching across the universe, lays down the law of time equally for all. In this world, a second is a second is a second. Time paces forward with exquisite regularity, at precisely the same velocity in every corner of space. Time is an infinite ruler. Time is absolute.

Every afternoon, the townspeople of Berne convene at the west end of Kramgasse. There, at four minutes to three, the Zytgloggeturm pays tribute to time. High on the turret of the tower clowns dance, roosters crow, bears play fife and drum, their mechanical movements and sounds synchronized exactly by the turning of gears, which, in turn, are inspired by the perfection of time. At three o'clock precisely, a massive bell chimes three times, people verify their watches and then return to their offices on Speichergasse, their shops on Marktgasse, their farms beyond the bridges on the Aare.

Those of religious faith see time as the evidence for God. For surely nothing could be created perfect without a Creator. Nothing could be universal and not be divine. All absolutes are part of the One Absolute. And wherever absolutes, so too time. Thus the philosophers of ethics have placed time at the center of their belief. Time is the reference against which all actions are judged. Time is the clarity for seeing right and wrong.

In a linen shop on Amthausgasse, a woman talks with her friend. She has just lost her job. For twenty years she worked as a clerk in the Bundeshaus, recording debates. She has supported her family. Now, with a daughter still in school and a husband who spends two hours each morning on the toilet, she has been fired. Her administrator, a heavily oiled and grotesque lady, came in one morning and told her to clear out her desk by the following day. The friend in the shop listens quietly, neatly folds the tablecloth she has purchased, picks lint off the sweater of the woman who has just lost her job. The two friends agree to meet for tea at ten o'clock the next morning. Ten o'clock. Seventeen hours and fifty-three minutes from this moment. The woman who has just lost her job smiles for the first time in days. In her mind she imagines the clock on the wall in her kitchen, ticking off each second between now and tomorrow at ten, without interruption, without consultation. And a similar clock in the home of her friend, synchronized. At twenty minutes to ten tomorrow morning, the woman will put on her scarf and her gloves and her coat and walk down the Schifflaube, past the Nydegg Bridge and on to the tea shop on Postgasse. Across town, at fifteen minutes before ten, her friend will leave her own house on Zeughausgasse and make her way to the same place. At ten o'clock they will meet. They will meet at ten o'clock.

A world in which time is absolute is a world of consolation. For while the movements of people are unpredictable, the movement of time is predictable. While people can be doubted, time cannot be doubted. While people brood, time skips ahead without looking back. In the coffeehouses, in the government buildings, in boats on Lake Geneva, people look at their watches and take refuge in time. Each person knows that somewhere is recorded the moment she was born, the moment she took her first step, the moment of her first passion, the moment she said goodbye to her parents.

• 3 MAY 1905

Consider a world in which cause and effect are erratic. Some-times the first precedes the second, sometimes the second the first. Or perhaps cause lies forever in the past while effect in the future, but future and past are entwined.

On the terrace of the Bundesterrasse is a striking view: the river Aare below and the Bernese Alps above. A man stands there just now, absently emptying his pockets and weeping. Without reason, his friends have abandoned him. No one calls any more, no one meets him for supper or beer at the tavern, no one invites him to their home. For twenty years he has been the ideal friend to his friends, generous, interested, soft-spoken, affectionate. What could have happened? A week from this moment on the terrace, the same man begins acting the goat, insulting everyone, wearing smelly clothes, stingy with money, allowing no one to come to his apartment on Laupenstrasse. Which was cause and which effect, which future and which past?

In Zürich, strict laws have recently been approved by the Council. Pistols may not be sold to the public. Banks and trading houses must be audited. All visitors, whether entering Zürich by boat on the river Limmat or by rail on the Selnau line, must be searched for contraband. The civil military is doubled. One month after the crackdown, Zürich is ripped by the worst crimes in its history. In daylight, people are murdered in the Weinplatz, paintings are stolen from the Kunsthaus, liquor is drunk in the pews of the Münsterhof. Are these criminal acts not misplaced in time? Or perhaps the new laws were action rather than reaction?

A young woman sits near a fountain in the Botanischer Garten. She comes here every Sunday to smell the white double violets, the musk rose, the matted pink gillyflowers. Suddenly, her heart soars, she blushes, she paces anxiously, she becomes happy for no reason. Days later, she meets a young man and is smitten with love. Are the two events not connected? But by what bizarre connection, by what twist in time, by what reversed logic?

In this acausal world, scientists are helpless. Their predictions become postdictions. Their equations become justifications, their logic, illogic. Scientists turn reckless and mutter like gamblers who cannot stop betting. Scientists are buffoons, not because they are rational but because the cosmos is irrational. Or perhaps it is not because the cosmos is irrational but because they are rational. Who can say which, in an acausal world?

In this world, artists are joyous. Unpredictability is the life of their paintings, their music, their novels. They delight in events not forecasted, happenings without explanation, retrospective.

Most people have learned how to live in the moment. The argument goes that if the past has uncertain effect on the present, there is no need to dwell on the past. And if the present has little effect on the future, present actions need not be weighed for their consequence. Rather, each act is an island in time, to be judged on its own. Families comfort a dying uncle not because of a likely inheritance, but because he is loved at that moment. Employees are hired not because of their résumés, but because of their good sense in interviews. Clerks trampled by their bosses fight back at each insult, with no fear for their future. It is a world of impulse. It is a world of sincerity. It is a world in which every word spoken speaks just to that moment, every glance given has only one meaning, each touch has no past or no future, each kiss is a kiss of immediacy.

• 4 May 1905

It is evening. Two couples, Swiss and English, sit at their usual table in the dining room of the Hotel San Murezzan in St. Moritz. They meet here yearly, for the month of June, to socialize and take the waters. The men are handsome in their black ties and their cummerbunds, the women beautiful in their evening gowns. The waiter walks across the fine wood floor, takes their orders.

"I gather the weather will be fair tomorrow," says the woman with the brocade in her hair. "That will be a relief." The others nod. "The baths do seem so much more pleasant when it's sunny. Although I suppose it shouldn't matter."

"Running Lightly is four-to-one in Dublin," says the admiral. "I'd back him if I had the money." He winks at his wife.

"I'll give you five-to-one if you're game," says the other man.

The women break their dinner rolls, butter them, carefully place their knives on the side of the butter plates. The men keep their eyes on the entrance.

"I love the lace of the serviettes," says the woman with the brocade in her hair. She takes her napkin and unfolds it, then folds it again.

"You say that every year, Josephine," the other woman says and smiles.

Dinner comes. Tonight, they dine on lobster Bordelaise, asparagus, steak, white wine.

"How is yours done?" says the woman with the brocade, looking at her husband.

"Splendidly. And yours?"

"A bit spicy. Like last week's."

"And, Admiral, how's the steak?"

"Never turned down a side of beef," says the admiral happily.

"Wouldn't notice you've been at the larder much," says the other man. "You've not put on one kilo since last year, or even for the last ten."

"Perhaps you can't notice, but she can," says the admiral, and winks at his wife.

"I may be mistaken, but it seems the rooms are a bit draftier this year," says the admiral's wife. The others nod, continue eating the lobster and the steak. "I always sleep best in cool rooms, but if it's drafty I wake up with a cough."

"Put the sheet over your head," says the other woman.

The admiral's wife says yes but looks puzzled.

"Tuck your head under the sheet and the draft won't bother you," repeats the other woman. "It happens to me all the time in Grindelwald. I have a window by my bed. I can leave it open if I put the sheet over my nose. Keeps the cold air out."

The woman with the brocade shifts in her chair, uncrosses her legs beneath the table.

Coffee comes. The men retire to the smoking room, the women to the wicker swing on the great deck outside.

"And how's the business since last year?" asks the admiral.

"Can't complain," says the other man, sipping his brandy.

"The children?"

"Grown a year."

On the porch, the women swing and look into the night.

And it is just the same in every hotel, in every house, in every town. For in this world, time does pass, but little happens. Just as little happens from year to year, little happens from month to month, day to day. If time and the passage of events are the same, then time moves barely at all. If time and events are not the same, then it is only people who barely move. If a person holds no ambitions in this world, he suffers unknowingly. If a person holds ambitions, he suffers knowingly, but very slowly.

• INTERLUDE

Einstein and Besso walk slowly down Speichergasse in the late afternoon. It is a quiet time of day. Shopkeepers are dropping their awnings and getting out their bicycles. From a second-floor window, a mother calls to her daughter to come home and prepare dinner.

Einstein has been explaining to his friend Besso why he wants to know time. But he says nothing of his dreams. Soon they will be at Besso's house. Sometimes Einstein stays there through dinner, and Mileva has to come get him, toting their infant. That usually happens when Einstein is possessed with a new project, as he is now, and all through dinner he twitches his leg under the table. Einstein isn't good dinner company.

Einstein leans over to Besso, who is also short, and says, "I want to understand time because I want to get close to The Old One."

Besso nods in accord. But there are problems, which Besso points out. For one, perhaps The Old One is not interested in getting close to his creations, intelligent or not. For another, it is not obvious that knowledge is closeness. For yet another, this time project could be too big for a twenty-six-year-old.

On the other hand, Besso thinks that his friend might be capable of anything. Already this year, Einstein has completed his Ph.D. thesis, finished one paper on photons and another on Brownian motion. The current project actually began as an investigation of electricity and magnetism, which, Einstein suddenly announced one day, would require a reconception of time. Besso is dazzled by Einstein's ambition.

For a while, Besso leaves Einstein alone with his thoughts. He wonders what Anna has cooked for dinner and looks down a side street where a silver boat on the Aare glints in the low sun. As the two men walk, their footsteps softly click on the cobblestones. They have known each other since their student days in Zürich.

"Got a letter from my brother in Rome," says Besso. "He's coming to visit for a month. Anna likes him because he always compliments her figure." Einstein smiles absently. "I won't be able to see you after work while my brother is here. Will you be all right?"

"What?" asks Einstein.

"I won't be able to see you much while my brother is here," repeats Besso. "Will you be all right by yourself?"

"Sure," says Einstein. "Don't worry about me."

Ever since Besso has known him, Einstein has been self-sufficient. His family moved around when he was growing up. Like Besso, he is married, but he hardly goes anywhere with his wife. Even at home, he sneaks away from Mileva in the middle of the night and goes to the kitchen to calculate long pages of equations, which he shows Besso the next day at the office.

Besso eyes his friend curiously. For such a recluse and an introvert, this passion for closeness seems odd.

• 8 May 1905

The world will end on 26 September 1907. Everyone knows it.

In Berne, it is just as in all cities and towns. One year before the end, schools close their doors. Why learn for the future, with so brief a future? Delighted to have lessons finished forever, children play hide-and-seek in the arcades of Kramgasse, run down Aarstrasse and skip stones on the river, squander their coins on peppermint and licorice. Their parents let them do what they wish.

One month before the end, businesses close. The Bundeshaus halts its proceedings. The federal telegraph building on Speichergasse falls silent. Likewise the watch factory on Laupenstrasse, the mill past the Nydegg Bridge. What need is there for commerce and industry with so little time left?

At the outdoor cafés on Amthausgasse, people sit and sip coffee and talk easily of their lives. A liberation fills the air. Just now, for example, a woman with brown eyes is speaking to her mother about how little time they spent together in her childhood, when the mother worked as a seamstress. The mother and daughter are now planning a trip to Lucerne. They will fit two lives into the little time remaining. At another table, a man tells a friend about a hated supervisor who often made love to the man's wife in the office coatroom after hours and threatened to fire him if he or his wife caused any trouble. But what is there to fear now? The man has settled with the supervisor and reconciled with his wife. Relieved at last, he stretches his legs and lets his eyes roam over the Alps.

At the bakery on Marktgasse, the thick-fingered baker puts dough in the oven and sings. These days people are polite when they order their bread. They smile and pay promptly, for money is losing its value. They chat about picnics in Fribourg, cherished time listening to their children's stories, long walks in mid-afternoon. They do not seem to mind that the world will soon end, because everyone shares the same fate. A world with one month is a world of equality.

One day before the end, the streets swirl in laughter. Neighbors who have never spoken greet each other as friends, strip off their clothing and bathe in the fountains. Others dive in the Aare. After swimming until exhausted, they lie in the thick grass along the river and read poetry. A barrister and a postal clerk who have never before met walk arm in arm through the Botanischer Garten, smile at the cyclamens and asters, discuss art and color. What do their past stations matter? In a world of one day they are equal.

In the shadows of a side street off Aarbergergasse, a man and a woman lean against a wall, drink beer, and eat smoked beef. Afterwards, she will take him to her apartment. She is married to someone else, but for years she has wanted this man, and she will satisfy her wants on this last day of the world.

A few souls gallop through the streets doing good deeds, attempting to correct their misdeeds of the past. Theirs are the only unnatural smiles.

One minute before the end of the world, everyone gathers on the grounds of the Kunstmuseum. Men, women, and children form a giant circle and hold hands. No one moves. No one speaks. It is so absolutely quiet that each person can hear the heartbeat of the person to his right or his left. This is the last minute of the world. In the absolute silence a purple gentian in the garden catches the light on the underside of its blossom, glows for a moment, then dissolves among the other flowers. Behind the museum, the needled leaves of a larch gently shudder as a breeze moves through the tree. Farther back, through the forest, the Aare reflects sunlight, bends the light with each ripple on its skin. To the east, the tower of St. Vincent's rises into sky, red and fragile, its stonework as delicate as veins of a leaf. And higher up, the Alps, snow-tipped, blending white and purple, large and silent. A cloud floats in the sky. A sparrow flutters. No one speaks.

In the last seconds, it is as if everyone has leaped off Topaz Peak, holding hands. The end approaches like approaching ground. Cool air rushes by, bodies are weightless. The silent horizon yawns for miles. And below, the vast blanket of snow hurtles nearer and nearer to envelop this circle of pinkness and life.

It is late afternoon, and, for a brief moment, the sun nestles in a snowy hollow of the Alps, fire touching ice. The long slants of light sweep from the mountains, cross a restful lake, cast shadows in a town below.

In many ways, it is a town of one piece and a whole. Spruce and larch and arolla pine form a gentle border north and west, while higher up are fire lilies, purple gentians, alpine columbines. In pastures near the town graze cattle for making butter, cheese, and chocolate. A little textile mill produces silks, ribbons, cotton clothes. A church bell rings. The smell of smoked beef fills the streets and alleyways.

On closer look, it is a town in many pieces. One neighborhood lives in the fifteenth century. Here, the storeys of the rough-stone houses are joined by outdoor stairs and galleries, while the upper gables gape and open to the winds. Moss grows between the stone slabs of the roofs. Another section of the village is a picture of the eighteenth century. Burnt red tiles lie angled on the straight-lined roofs. A church has oval windows, corbeled loggias, granite parapets. Another section holds the present, with arcades lining every avenue, metal railings on the balconies, façades made of smooth sandstone. Each section of the village is fastened to a different time.

On this late afternoon, in these few moments while the sun is nestled in a snowy hollow of the Alps, a person could sit beside the lake and contemplate the texture of time. Hypothetically, time might be smooth or rough, prickly or silky, hard or soft. But in this world, the texture of time happens to be sticky. Portions of towns become stuck in some moment in history and do not get out. So, too, individual people become stuck in some point of their lives and do not get free.

Just now, a man in one of the houses below the mountains is

talking to a friend. He is talking of his school days at the gymnasium. His certificates of excellence in mathematics and history hang on the walls, his sporting medals and trophies occupy the bookshelves. Here, on a table, is a photograph of him as captain of the fencing team, embraced by other young men who have since gone to university, become engineers and bankers, gotten married. There, in the dresser, his clothes from twenty years, the fencing blouse, the tweed pants now too close around the waist. The friend, who has been trying for years to introduce the man to other friends, nods courteously, struggles silently to breathe in the tiny room.

In another house, a man sits alone at his table, laid out for two. Ten years ago, he sat here across from his father, was unable to say that he loved him, searched through the years of his childhood for some moment of closeness, remembered the evenings that silent man sat alone with his book, was unable to say that he loved him, was unable to say that he loved him. The table is set with two plates, two glasses, two forks, as on that last night. The man begins to eat, cannot eat, weeps uncontrollably. He never said that he loved him.

In another house, a woman looks fondly at a photograph of her son, young and smiling and bright. She writes to him at a long-defunct address, imagines the happy letters back. When her son knocks at the door, she does not answer. When her son, with his puffy face and glassy eyes, calls up to her window for money, she does not hear him. When her son, with his stumbling walk, leaves notes for her, begging to see her, she throws out the notes unopened. When her son stands in the night outside her house, she goes to bed early. In the morning, she looks at his photograph, writes adoring letters to a long-defunct address.

A spinster sees the face of the young man who loved her in the mirror of her bedroom, on the ceiling of the bakery, on the surface of the lake, in the sky.

The tragedy of this world is that no one is happy, whether stuck in a time of pain or of joy. The tragedy of this world is that everyone is alone. For a life in the past cannot be shared with the present. Each person who gets stuck in time gets stuck alone.

· 11 MAY 1905

Walking on the Marktgasse, one sees a wondrous sight. The cherries in the fruit stalls sit aligned in rows, the hats in the millinery shop are neatly stacked, the flowers on the balconies are arranged in perfect symmetries, no crumbs lie on the bakery floor, no milk is spilled on the cobblestones of the buttery. No thing is out of place.

When a gay party leaves a restaurant, the tables are more tidy than before. When a wind blows gently through the street, the street is swept clean, the dirt and dust transported to the edge of town. When waves of water splash against the shore, the shore rebuilds itself. When leaves fall from the trees, the leaves line up like birds in V-formation. When clouds form faces, the faces stay. When a pipe lets smoke into a room, the soot drifts toward a corner of the room, leaving clear air. Painted balconies exposed to wind and rain become brighter in time. The sound of thunder makes a broken vase reform itself, makes the fractured shards leap up to the precise positions where they fit and bind. The fragrant odor of a passing cinnamon cart intensifies, not dissipates, with time.

Do these happenings seem strange?

In this world, the passage of time brings increasing order. Order is the law of nature, the universal trend, the cosmic direction. If time is an arrow, that arrow points toward order. The future is pattern, organization, union, intensification; the past, randomness, confusion, disintegration, dissipation.

Philosophers have argued that without a trend toward order, time would lack meaning. The future would be indistinguishable from the past. Sequences of events would be just so many random scenes from a thousand novels. History would be indistinct, like the mist slowly gathered by treetops in evening.

In such a world, people with untidy houses lie in their beds and wait for the forces of nature to jostle the dust from their windowsills and straighten the shoes in their closets. People with untidy affairs may picnic while their calendars become organized, their appointments arranged, their accounts balanced. Lipsticks and brushes and letters may be tossed into purses with the satisfaction that they will sort themselves out automatically. Gardens need never be pruned, weeds never uprooted. Desks become neat by the end of the day. Clothes on the floor in the evening lie on chairs in the morning. Missing socks reappear.

If one visits a city in spring, one sees another wondrous sight. For in springtime the populace become sick of the order in their lives. In spring, people furiously lay waste to their houses. They sweep in dirt, smash chairs, break windows. On Aarbergergasse, or any residential avenue in spring, one hears the sounds of broken glass, shouting, howling, laughter. In spring, people meet at unarranged times, burn their appointment books, throw away their watches, drink through the night. This hysterical abandon continues until summer, when people regain their senses and return to order.

• 14 May 1905

There is a place where time stands still. Raindrops hang motionless in air. Pendulums of clocks float mid-swing. Dogs raise their muzzles in silent howls. Pedestrians are frozen on the dusty streets, their legs cocked as if held by strings. The aromas of dates, mangoes, coriander, cumin are suspended in space.

As a traveler approaches this place from any direction, he moves more and more slowly. His heartbeats grow farther apart, his breathing slackens, his temperature drops, his thoughts diminish, until he reaches dead center and stops. For this is the center of time. From this place, time travels outward in concentric circles—at rest at the center, slowly picking up speed at greater diameters.

Who would make pilgrimage to the center of time? Parents with children, and lovers.

And so, at the place where time stands still, one sees parents clutching their children, in a frozen embrace that will never let go. The beautiful young daughter with blue eyes and blond hair will never stop smiling the smile she smiles now, will never lose this soft pink glow on her cheeks, will never grow wrinkled or tired, will never get injured, will never unlearn what her parents have taught her, will never think thoughts that her parents don't know, will never know evil, will never tell her parents that she does not love them, will never leave her room with the view of the ocean, will never stop touching her parents as she does now.

And at the place where time stands still, one sees lovers kissing in the shadows of buildings, in a frozen embrace that will never let go. The loved one will never take his arms from where they are now, will never give back the bracelet of memories, will never journey far from his lover, will never place himself in danger in self-sacrifice, will never fail to show his love, will never become jealous, will never fall in love with someone else, will never lose the passion of this instant in time.

One must consider that these statues are illuminated by only the most feeble red light, for light is diminished almost to nothing at the center of time, its vibrations slowed to echoes in vast canyons, its intensity reduced to the faint glow of fireflies.

Those not quite at dead center do indeed move, but at the pace of glaciers. A brush of the hair might take a year, a kiss might take a thousand. While a smile is returned, seasons pass in the outer world. While a child is hugged, bridges rise. While a goodbye is said, cities crumble and are forgotten.

And those who return to the outer world . . . Children grow rapidly, forget the centuries-long embrace from their parents, which to them lasted but seconds. Children become adults, live far from their parents, live in their own houses, learn ways of their own, suffer pain, grow old. Children curse their parents for trying to hold them forever, curse time for their own wrinkled skin and hoarse voices. These now old children also want to stop time, but at another time. They want to freeze their own children at the center of time.

Lovers who return find their friends are long gone. After all, lifetimes have passed. They move in a world they do not recognize. Lovers who return still embrace in the shadows of buildings, but now their embraces seem empty and alone. Soon they forget the centuries-long promises, which to them lasted only seconds. They become jealous even among strangers, say hateful things to each other, lose passion, drift apart, grow old and alone in a world they do not know.

Some say it is best not to go near the center of time. Life is a vessel of sadness, but it is noble to live life, and without time there is no life. Others disagree. They would rather have an eternity of contentment, even if that eternity were fixed and frozen, like a butterfly mounted in a case.

Imagine a world in which there is no time. Only images.

A child at the seashore, spellbound by her first glimpse of the ocean. A woman standing on a balcony at dawn, her hair down, her loose sleeping silks, her bare feet, her lips. The curved arch of the arcade near the Zähringer Fountain on Kramgasse, sandstone and iron. A man sitting in the quiet of his study, holding the photograph of a woman, a pained look on his face. An osprey framed in the sky, its wings outstretched, the sun rays piercing between feathers. A young boy sitting in an empty auditorium, his heart racing as if he were on stage. Footprints in snow on a winter island. A boat on the water at night, its lights dim in the distance, like a small red star in the black sky. A locked cabinet of pills. A leaf on the ground in autumn, red and gold and brown, delicate. A woman crouching in the bushes, waiting by the house of her estranged husband, whom she must talk to. A soft rain on a spring day, on a walk that is the last walk a young man will take in the place that he loves. Dust on a windowsill. A stall of peppers on Marktgasse, the yellow and green and red. Matterhorn, the jagged peak of white pushing into the solid blue sky, the green valley and the log cabins. The eye of a needle. Dew on leaves, crystal, opalescent. A mother on her bed, weeping, the smell of basil in the air. A child on a bicycle in the Kleine Schanze, smiling the smile of a lifetime. A tower of prayer, tall and octagonal, open balcony, solemn, surrounded by arms. Steam rising from a lake in early morning. An open drawer. Two friends at a café, the lamplight illuminating one friend's face, the other in shadow. A cat watching a bug on the window. A young woman on a bench, reading a letter, tears of joy in her green eyes. A great field, lined with cedar and spruce. Sunlight, in long angles through the window in late afternoon. A massive tree fallen, roots sprawling in air, bark, limbs still green. The white of a sailboat, with the wind behind it, sails billowed like wings of a giant white bird. A father and son alone at a restaurant, the father sad and staring down at the tablecloth. An oval window, looking out on fields of hay, a wooden cart, cows, green and purple in the afternoon light. A broken bottle on the floor, brown liquid in the crevices, a woman with red eyes. An old man in the kitchen, cooking breakfast for his grandson, the boy gazing out the window at a white painted bench. A worn book lying on a table beside a dim lamp. The white on water as a wave breaks, blown by wind. A woman lying on her couch with wet hair, holding the hand of a man she will never see again. A train with red cars, on a great stone bridge with graceful arches, a river underneath, tiny dots that are houses in the distance. Dust motes floating in sunlight through a window. The thin skin in the middle of a neck, thin enough to see the pulse of blood underneath. A man and woman naked, wrapped around each other. The blue shadows of trees in a full moon. The top of a mountain with a strong steady wind, the valley falling away on all sides, sandwiches of beef and cheese. A child wincing from his father's slap, the father's lips twisted in anger, the child not understanding. A strange face in the mirror, gray at the temples. A young man holding a telephone, startled at what he is hearing. A family photograph, the parents young and relaxed, the children in ties and dresses and smiling. A tiny light, far through a thicket of trees. The red at sunset. An eggshell, white, fragile, unbroken. A blue hat washed up on shore. Roses cut and adrift on the river beneath the bridge, with a château rising. Red hair of a lover, wild, mischievous, promising. The purple petals of an iris, held by a young woman. A room of four walls, two windows, two beds, a table, a lamp, two people with red faces, tears. The first kiss. Planets caught in space, oceans, silence. A bead of water on the window. A coiled rope. A yellow brush.

• 20 May 1905

A glance along the crowded booths on Spitalgasse tells the story. The shoppers walk hesitantly from one stall to the next, discovering what each shop sells. Here is tobacco, but where is mustard seed? Here are sugar beets, but where is cod? Here is goat's milk, but where is sassafras? These are not tourists in Berne on their first visit. These are the citizens of Berne. Not a man can remember that two days back he bought chocolate at a shop named Ferdinand's, at no. 17, or beef at the Hof delicatessen, at no. 36. Each shop and its specialty must be found anew. Many walk with maps, directing the map-holders from one arcade to the next in the city they have lived in all their lives, in the street they have traveled for years. Many walk with notebooks, to record what they have learned while it is briefly in their heads. For in this world, people have no memories.

When it is time to return home at the end of the day, each person consults his address book to learn where he lives. The butcher, who has made some unattractive cuts in his one day of butchery, discovers that his home is no. 29 Nägeligasse. The stockbroker, whose short-term memory of the market has produced some excellent investments, reads that he now lives at no. 89 Bundesgasse. Arriving home, each man finds a woman and children waiting at the door, introduces himself, helps with the evening meal, reads stories to his children. Likewise, each woman returning from her job meets a husband, children, sofas, lamps, wallpaper, china patterns. Late at night, the wife and husband do not linger at the table to discuss the day's activities, their children's school, the bank account. Instead, they smile at one another, feel the warming blood, the ache between the legs as when they met the first time fifteen years ago. They find their bedroom, stumble past family photographs they do not recognize, and pass the night in lust. For it is only habit and memory that dulls the physical passion. Without memory, each night is the first night, each morning is the first morning, each kiss and touch are the first.

A world without memory is a world of the present. The past exists only in books, in documents. In order to know himself, each person carries his own Book of Life, which is filled with the history of his life. By reading its pages daily, he can relearn the identity of his parents, whether he was born high or born low, whether he did well or did poorly in school, whether he has accomplished anything in his life. Without his Book of Life, a person is a snapshot, a two-dimensional image, a ghost. In the leafy cafés on the Brunngasshalde, one hears anguished shrieking from a man who just read that he once killed another man, sighs from a woman who just discovered she was courted by a prince, sudden boasting from a woman who has learned that she received top honors from her university ten years prior. Some pass the twilight hours at their tables reading from their Books of Life; others frantically fill its extra pages with the day's events.

With time, each person's Book of Life thickens until it cannot be read in its entirety. Then comes a choice. Elderly men and women may read the early pages, to know themselves as youths; or they may read the end, to know themselves in later years.

Some have stopped reading altogether. They have abandoned the past. They have decided that it matters not if yesterday they were rich or poor, educated or ignorant, proud or humble, in love or empty-hearted—no more than it matters how a soft wind gets into their hair. Such people look you directly in the eye and grip your hand firmly. Such people walk with the limber stride of their youth. Such people have learned how to live in a world without memory.

• 22 MAY 1905

Dawn. A salmon fog floats through the city, carried on the breath of the river. The sun waits beyond the Nydegg Bridge, throws its long, reddened spikes along Kramgasse to the giant clock that measures time, illuminates the underside of balconies. Sounds of morning drift through the streets like the smell of bread. A child wakes and cries for her mother. An awning creaks quietly as the milliner arrives at his shop on Marktgasse. An engine whines on the river. Two women talk softly beneath an arcade.

As the city melts through fog and the night, one sees a strange sight. Here an old bridge is half-finished. There, a house has been removed from its foundations. Here, a street veers east for no obvious reason. There, a bank sits in the middle of the grocery market. The lower stained-glass windows of St. Vincent's portray religious themes, the uppers switch abruptly to a picture of the Alps in spring. A man walks briskly toward the Bundeshaus, stops suddenly, puts his hands to his head, shouts excitedly, turns, and hurries in the opposite direction.

This is a world of changed plans, of sudden opportunities, of unexpected visions. For in this world, time flows not evenly but fitfully and, as consequence, people receive fitful glimpses of the future.

When a mother receives a sudden vision of where her son will live, she moves her house to be near him. When a builder sees the place of commerce in the future, he twists his road in that direction. When a child briefly glimpses herself as a florist, she decides not to attend university. When a young man gets a vision of the woman he will marry, he waits for her. When a solicitor catches sight of himself in the robes of a judge in Zürich, he abandons his job in Berne. Indeed, what sense is there in continuing the present when one has seen the future?

For those who have had their vision, this is a world of guaranteed success. Few projects are started that do not advance a career. Few trips are taken that do not lead to the city of destiny. Few friends are made who will not be friends in the future. Few passions are wasted.

For those who have not had their vision, this is a world of inactive suspense. How can one enroll in university without knowing one's future occupation? How can one set up an apothecary on Marktgasse when a similar shop might do better on Spitalgasse? How can one make love to a man when he may not remain faithful? Such people sleep most of the day and wait for their vision to come.

Thus, in this world of brief scenes from the future, few risks are taken. Those who have seen the future do not need to take risks, and those who have not yet seen the future wait for their vision without taking risks.

Some few who have witnessed the future do all they can to refute it. A man goes to tend the museum gardens in Neuchâtel after he has seen himself a barrister in Lucerne. A youth embarks on a vigorous sailing voyage with his father after a vision that his father will die soon of heart trouble. A young woman allows herself to fall in love with one man even though she has seen that she will marry another. Such people stand on their balconies at twilight and shout that the future can be changed, that thousands of futures are possible. In time, the gardener in Neuchâtel gets tired of his low wages, becomes a barrister in Lucerne. The father dies of his heart, and his son hates himself for not forcing his father to keep to his bed. The young woman is deserted by her lover, marries a man who will let her have solitude with her pain.

Who would fare better in this world of fitful time? Those who have seen the future and live only one life? Or those who have not seen the future and wait to live life? Or those who deny the future and live two lives?

A man or a woman suddenly thrust into this world would have to dodge houses and buildings. For all is in motion. Houses and apartments, mounted on wheels, go careening through Bahnhofplatz and race through the narrows of Marktgasse, their occupants shouting from second-floor windows. The Post Bureau doesn't remain on Postgasse, but flies through the city on rails, like a train. Nor does the Bundeshaus sit quietly on Bundesgasse. Everywhere the air whines and roars with the sound of motors and locomotion. When a person comes out of his front door at sunrise, he hits the ground running, catches up with his office building, hurries up and down flights of stairs, works at a desk propelled in circles, gallops home at the end of the day. No one sits under a tree with a book, no one gazes at the ripples on a pond, no one lies in thick grass in the country. No one is still.

Why such a fixation on speed? Because in this world time passes more slowly for people in motion. Thus everyone travels at high velocity, to gain time.

The speed effect was not noticed until the invention of the internal combustion engine and the beginnings of rapid transportation. On 8 September 1889, Mr. Randolph Whig of Surrey took his mother-in-law to London at high speed in his new motor car. To his delight, he arrived in half the expected time, a conversation having scarcely begun, and decided to look into the phenomenon. After his researches were published, no one went slowly again.

Since time is money, financial considerations alone dictate that each brokerage house, each manufacturing plant, each grocer's shop constantly travel as rapidly as possible, to achieve advantage over their competitors. Such buildings are fitted with giant engines of propulsion and are never at rest.

Their motors and crankshafts roar far more loudly than the equipment and people inside them.

Likewise, houses are sold not just on their size and design, but also on speed. For the faster a house travels, the more slowly the clocks tick inside and the more time available to its occupants. Depending on the speed, a person in a fast house could gain several minutes on his neighbors in a single day. This obsession with speed carries through the night, when valuable time could be lost, or gained, while asleep. At night, the streets are ablaze with lights, so that passing houses might avoid collisions, which are always fatal. At night, people dream of speed, of youth, of opportunity.

In this world of great speed, one fact has been only slowly appreciated. By logical tautology, the motional effect is all relative. Because when two people pass on the street, each perceives the other in motion, just as a man in a train perceives the trees to fly by his window. Consequently, when two people pass on the street, each sees the other's time flow more slowly. Each sees the other gaining time. This reciprocity is maddening. More maddening still, the faster one travels past a neighbor, the faster the neighbor appears to be traveling.

Frustrated and despondent, some people have stopped looking out their windows. With the shades drawn, they never know how fast they are moving, how fast their neighbors and competitors are moving. They rise in the morning, take baths, eat plaited bread and ham, work at their desks, listen to music, talk to their children, lead lives of satisfaction.

Some argue that only the giant clock tower on Kramgasse keeps the true time, that it alone is at rest. Others point out that even the giant clock is in motion when viewed from the river Aare, or from a cloud.

Einstein and Besso sit at an outdoor café on Amthausgasse. It is noon, and Besso has talked his friend into leaving the office and getting some air.

"You don't look so good," says Besso.

Einstein shrugs his shoulders, almost embarrassed. Minutes go by, or perhaps only seconds.

"I'm making progress," says Einstein.

"I can tell," says Besso, studying with alarm the dark circles under his friend's eyes. It is also possible that Einstein has stopped eating again. Besso remembers when he looked just like Einstein does now, but for a different reason. It was in Zürich. Besso's father died suddenly, in his late forties. Besso, who had never gotten along with his father, felt grief-stricken and guilty. His studies came to a halt. To Besso's surprise, Einstein brought him into his lodgings and took care of him for a month.

Besso sees Einstein now and wishes he could help, but of course Einstein does not need help. To Besso, Einstein is without pain. He seems oblivious of his body and the world.

"I'm making progress," Einstein says again. "I think the secrets will come. Did you see the paper by Lorentz I left on your desk?"

"Ugly."

"Yes. Ugly and ad hoc. It couldn't possibly be right. The electromagnetic experiments are telling us something much more fundamental." Einstein scratches his mustache and hungrily eats the crackers on the table.

For some time the two men are silent. Besso puts four cubes of sugar in his coffee while Einstein gazes at the Bernese Alps, far off in the distance and barely visible through the haze. In actuality, Einstein is looking through the Alps, into space. He sometimes gets migraines from such farsighted vision and must then lie on his green slip-covered sofa with his eyes closed.

"Anna wants you and Mileva to come for dinner next week," says Besso. "You can bring the baby if you need to." Einstein nods.

Besso has another coffee, sights a young woman at a neighboring table and tucks in his shirt. He is almost as disheveled as Einstein, who by this time is staring at galaxies. Besso indeed worries about his friend, although he has seen him this way in the past. Perhaps the dinner will be a diversion.

"Saturday night," says Besso.

"I'm engaged Saturday night," Einstein says unexpectedly. "But Mileva and Hans Albert can come."

Besso laughs and says, "Saturday night at eight." He is puzzled why his friend ever got married in the first place. Einstein himself can't explain it. He once admitted to Besso that he had hoped Mileva would at least do the housework, but it hasn't worked out that way. The unmade bed, the dirty laundry, the piles of dishes are just as before. And there have been even more chores with the baby.

"What did you think about the Rasmussen application?" asks Besso.

"The bottle centrifuge?"

"Yes."

"The shaft will vibrate too much to be useful," says Einstein, "but the idea is clever. I think it would work with a flexible mounting that could find its own rotation axis."

Besso knows what that means. Einstein will work up a new design himself and send it to Rasmussen without requesting payment or even acknowledgment. Often, the lucky recipients of Einstein's suggestions don't even know who revises their patent applications. Not that Einstein doesn't enjoy recognition. A few years ago, when he saw the issue of *Annalen der Physik* bearing his first paper, he imitated a rooster for fully five minutes.

A mushy, brown peach is lifted from the garbage and placed on the table to pinken. It pinkens, it turns hard, it is carried in a shopping sack to the grocer's, put on a shelf, removed and crated, returned to the tree with pink blossoms. In this world, time flows backward.

A withered woman sits in a chair hardly moving, her face red and swollen, her eyesight almost gone, her hearing gone, her breathing scratchy like the rustle of dead leaves on stones. Years pass. There are few visitors. Gradually, the woman gains strength, eats more, loses the heavy lines in her face. She hears voices, music. Vague shadows gather themselves into light and lines and images of tables, chairs, people's faces. The woman makes excursions from her small house, goes to the market, occasionally visits a friend, drinks tea at cafés in good weather. She takes needles and yarn from the bottom drawer of her dresser and crochets. She smiles when she likes her work. One day her husband, with whitened face, is carried into her house. In hours, his cheeks become pink, he stands stooped over, straightens out, speaks to her. Her house becomes their house. They eat meals together, tell jokes, laugh. They travel through the country, visit friends. Her white hair darkens with brown streaks, her voice resonates with new tones. She goes to a retirement party at the gymnasium, begins teaching history. She loves her students, argues with them after class. She reads during her lunch hour and at night. She meets friends and discusses history and current events. She helps her husband with the accounts at his chemist's store, walks with him at the foot of the mountains, makes love to him. Her skin becomes soft, her hair long and brown, her breasts firm. She sees her husband for the first time in the library of the university, returns his glances. She attends classes. She graduates from the gymnasium, with her parents and sister crying tears of happiness. She lives at home with her parents, spends hours with her mother walking through the woods by their house, helps with the dishes. She tells stories to her younger sister, is read to at night before bed, grows smaller. She crawls. She nurses.

A middle-aged man walks from the stage of an auditorium in Stockholm, holding a medal. He shakes hands with the president of the Swedish Academy of Sciences, receives the Nobel Prize for physics, listens to the glorious citation. The man thinks briefly about the award he is to receive. His thoughts quickly shift twenty years to the future, when he will work alone in a small room with only pencil and paper. Day and night he will work, making many false starts, filling the trash basket with unsuccessful chains of equations and logical sequences. But some evenings he will return to his desk knowing he has learned things about Nature that no one has ever known, ventured into the forest and found light, gotten hold of precious secrets. On those evenings, his heart will pound as if he were in love. The anticipation of that rush of the blood, that time when he will be young and unknown and unafraid of mistakes, overpowers him now as he sits in his chair in the auditorium in Stockholm, at great distance from the tiny voice of the president announcing his name.

A man stands at the graveside of his friend, throws a handful of dirt on the coffin, feels the cold April rain on his face. But he does not weep. He looks ahead to the day when his friend's lungs will be strong, when his friend will be out of his bed and laughing, when the two of them will drink ale together, go sailing, talk. He does not weep. He waits longingly for a particular day he remembers in the future when he and his friend will have sandwiches on a low flat table, when he will describe his fear of growing old and unloved and his friend will nod gently, when the rain will slide down the glass of the window.

• 3 June 1905

Imagine a world in which people live just one day. Either the rate of heartbeats and breathing is speeded up so that an entire lifetime is compressed to the space of one turn of the earth on its axis—or the rotation of the earth is slowed to such a low gear that one complete revolution occupies a whole human lifetime. Either interpretation is valid. In either case, a man or woman sees one sunrise, one sunset.

In this world, no one lives to witness the change of the seasons. A person born in December in any European country never sees the hyacinth, the lily, the aster, the cyclamen, the edelweiss, never sees the leaves of the maple turn red and gold, never hears the crickets or the warblers. A person born in December lives his life cold. Likewise, a person born in July never feels a snowflake on her cheek, never sees the crystal on a frozen lake, never hears the squeak of boots in fresh snow. A person born in July lives her life warm. The variety of seasons is learned about in books.

In this world, a life is planned by light. A person born at sunset spends the first half of his life in nighttime, learns indoor trades like weaving and watchmaking, reads a great deal, becomes intellectual, eats too much, is frightened of the vast dark outdoors, cultivates shadows. A person born at sunrise learns outdoor occupations like farming and masonry, becomes physically fit, avoids books and mental projects, is sunny and confident, is afraid of nothing.

Both sunset and sunrise babies flounder when the light changes. When sunrise comes, those born at sunset are overwhelmed by the sudden sight of trees and oceans and mountains, are blinded by daylight, return to their houses and cover their windows, spend the rest of their lives in half light. When sunset comes, those born at sunrise wail at the disappearance of birds in the sky, the layered shades of blue in the sea, the hypnotic movement of clouds. They wail and refuse to learn the dark crafts indoors, lie on the ground and look up and struggle to see what they once saw.

In this world in which a human life spans but a single day, people heed time like cats straining to hear sounds in the attic. For there is no time to lose. Birth, schooling, love affairs, marriage, profession, old age must all be fit within one transit of the sun, one modulation of light. When people pass on the street, they tip their hats and hurry on. When people meet at houses, they politely inquire of each other's health and then attend to their own affairs. When people gather at cafés, they nervously study the shifting of shadows and do not sit long. Time is too precious. A life is a moment in season. A life is one snowfall. A life is one autumn day. A life is the delicate, rapid edge of a closing door's shadow. A life is a brief movement of arms and of legs.

When old age comes, whether in light or in dark, a person discovers that he knows no one. There hasn't been time. Parents have passed away at midday or midnight. Brothers and sisters have moved to distant cities, to seize passing opportunities. Friends have changed with the changing angle of the sun.

Houses, towns, jobs, lovers have all been planned to accommodate a life framed in one day. A person in old age knows no one. He talks to people, but he does not know them. His life is scattered in fragments of conversation, forgotten by fragments of people. His life is divided into hasty episodes, witnessed by few. He sits at his bedside table, listens to the sound of his running bath, and wonders whether anything exists outside of his mind. Did that embrace from his mother really exist? Did that laughing rivalry with his school friend really exist? Did that first tingle of lovemaking really exist? Did his lover exist? Where are they now? Where are they now, as he sits at his bedside table, listening to the sound of his running bath, vaguely perceiving the change in the light.

• 5 June 1905

From a description of the location and appearance of rivers, trees, buildings, people, all would seem common. The Aare bends to the east, is sprinkled with boats carrying potatoes and sugar beets. Arolla pines dot the foothills of the Alps, the trees' cone-laden branches curving upward like arms of a candelabrum. Three-storey houses with red-tiled roofs and dormer windows sit quietly on Aarstrasse, overlooking the river. Shopkeepers on Marktgasse wave their arms at all passersby, hawking handkerchiefs, fine watches, tomatoes, sour bread, and fennel. The smell of smoked beef wafts down the avenues. A man and woman stand on their small balcony on Kramgasse, arguing and smiling while they argue. A young girl walks slowly through the garden at the Kleine Schanze. The large redwood door of the Post Bureau opens and closes, opens and closes. A dog barks.

But seen through the eyes of any one person the scene is quite different. For example, one woman sitting on the banks of the Aare sees the boats pass by at great speed, as if moving on skates across ice. To another, the boats appear sluggish, barely rounding the bend in the whole of the afternoon. A man standing on Aarstrasse looks at the river to discover that the boats travel first forwards, then backwards.

These discrepancies are repeated elsewhere. Just now a chemist is walking back to his shop on Kochergasse, having taken his noon meal. This is the picture he sees: two women gallop past him, churning their arms wildly and talking so rapidly that he cannot understand them. A solicitor runs across the street to an appointment somewhere, his head jerking this way and that like a small animal's. A ball tossed by a child from a balcony hurtles through the air like a bullet, a blur barely visible. The residents of no. 82, just glimpsed through their window, fly through the house from one room to the next, sit down for an instant, shovel down a meal in one minute, disappear, reappear. Clouds overhead come together, move apart, come together again with the pace of successive exhales and inhales.

On the other side of the street, the baker observes the same scene. He notes that two women leisurely stroll up the street, stop to talk to a solicitor, then walk on. The solicitor goes into an apartment at no. 82, sits down at a table for lunch, walks to the first-floor window where he catches a ball thrown by a child on the street.

To yet a third person standing under a lamppost on Kochergasse, the events have no movement at all: two women, a solicitor, a ball, a child, three barges, an apartment interior are captured like paintings in the bright summer light.

And it is similar with any sequence of events, in this world where time is a sense.

In a world where time is a sense, like sight or like taste, a sequence of episodes may be quick or may be slow, dim or intense, salty or sweet, causal or without cause, orderly or random, depending on the prior history of the viewer. Philosophers sit in cafés on Amthausgasse and argue whether time really exists outside human perception. Who can say if an event happens fast or slow, causally or without cause, in the past or the future? Who can say if events happen at all? The philosophers sit with half-opened eyes and compare their aesthetics of time.

Some few people are born without any sense of time. As consequence, their sense of place becomes heightened to excruciating degree. They lie in tall grass and are questioned by poets and painters from all over the world. These time-deaf are beseeched to describe the precise placement of trees in the spring, the shape of snow on the Alps, the angle of sun on a church, the position of rivers, the location of moss, the pattern of birds in a flock. Yet the time-deaf are unable to speak what they know. For speech needs a sequence of words, spoken in time.

• 9 JUNE 1905

Suppose that people live forever.

Strangely, the population of each city splits in two: the Laters and the Nows.

The Laters reason that there is no hurry to begin their classes at the university, to learn a second language, to read Voltaire or Newton, to seek promotion in their jobs, to fall in love, to raise a family. For all these things, there is an infinite span of time. In endless time, all things can be accomplished. Thus all things can wait. Indeed, hasty actions breed mistakes.

who can argue with their logic? The Laters can be recognized in any shop or promenade. They walk an easy gait and wear loose-fitting clothes. They take pleasure in reading whatever magazines are open, or rearranging furniture in their homes, or slipping into conversation the way a leaf falls from a tree. The Laters sit in cafés sipping coffee and discussing the possibilities of life.

The Nows note that with infinite lives, they can do all they can imagine. They will have an infinite number of careers, they will marry an infinite number of times, they will change their politics infinitely. Each person will be a lawyer, a bricklayer, a writer, an accountant, a painter, a physician, a farmer. The Nows are constantly reading new books, studying new trades, new languages. In order to taste the infinities of life, they begin early and never go slowly. And who can question their logic? The Nows are easily spotted. They are the owners of the cafés, the college professors, the doctors and nurses, the politicians, the people who rock their legs constantly whenever they sit down. They move through a succession of lives, eager to miss nothing. When two Nows chance to meet at the hexagonal pilaster of the Zähringer Fountain, they compare the lives they have mastered, exchange information, and glance at their watches. When two Laters meet at the same location, they ponder the future and follow the parabola of the water with their eyes.

The Nows and Laters have one thing in common. With infinite life comes an infinite list of relatives. Grandparents never die, nor do great-grandparents, great-aunts and great-uncles, great-great-aunts, and so on, back through the generations, all alive and offering advice. Sons never escape from the shadows of their fathers. Nor do daughters of their mothers. No one ever comes into his own.

When a man starts a business, he feels compelled to talk it over with his parents and grandparents and great-grandparents, ad infinitum, to learn from their errors. For no new enterprise is new. All things have been attempted by some antecedent in the family tree. Indeed, all things have been accomplished. But at a price. For in such a world, the multiplication of achievements is partly divided by the diminishment of ambition.

And when a daughter wants guidance from her mother, she cannot get it undiluted. Her mother must ask her mother, who must ask her mother, and so on forever. Just as sons and daughters cannot make decisions themselves, they cannot turn to parents for confident advice. Parents are not the source of certainty. There are one million sources.

Where every action must be verified one million times, life is ive. Bridges thrust halfway over rivers and then abruptly stop. Buildings rise nine stories high but have no roofs. The grocer's stocks of ginger, salt, cod, and beef change with every change of mind, every consultation. Sentences go unfinished. Engagements end just days before weddings. And on the avenues and streets, people turn their heads and peer behind their backs, to see who might be watching.

Such is the cost of immortality. No person is whole. No person is free. Over time, some have determined that the only way to live is to die. In death, a man or a woman is free of the weight of the past. These few souls, with their dear relatives looking on, dive into Lake Constance or hurl themselves from Monte Lema, ending their infinite lives. In this way, the finite has conquered the infinite, millions of autumns have yielded to no autumns, millions of snowfalls have yielded to no snowfalls, millions of admonitions have yielded to none.

• 10 June 1905

Suppose that time is not a quantity but a quality, like the luminescence of the night above the trees just when a rising moon has touched the treeline. Time exists, but it cannot be measured.

Just now, on a sunny afternoon, a woman stands in the middle of the Bahnhofplatz, waiting to meet a particular man. Some time ago, he saw her on the train to Fribourg, was entranced, and asked to take her to the Grosse Schanze gardens. From the urgency in his voice and the look in his eyes, the woman knew that he meant soon. So she waits for him, not impatiently, passing the time with a book. Some time later, perhaps on the following day, he arrives, they lock arms, walk to the gardens, stroll by the groupings of tulips, roses, martagon lilies, alpine columbines, sit on a white cedar bench for an unmeasurable time. Evening comes, marked by a change in the light, a reddening of the sky. The man and woman follow a winding path of small white stones to a restaurant on a hill. Have they been together a lifetime, or only a moment? Who can say?

Through the leaded windows of the restaurant, the mother of the man spots him sitting with the woman. She wrings her hands and whines, for she wants her son at home. She sees him as a child. Has any time passed since he lived at home, played catch with his father, rubbed his mother's back before bed? The mother sees that boyish laugh, caught in candlelight through the leaded windows of the restaurant, and she is certain that no time has passed, that her son, her child, belongs with her at home. She waits outside, wringing her hands, while her son grows older quickly in the intimacy of this evening, of this woman he has met.

Across the street, on Aarbergergasse, two men argue about a shipment of pharmaceuticals. The receiver is angry because the pharmaceuticals, which have a short shelf life, have arrived aged and inactive. He expected them long ago and, in fact, has been waiting for them at the train station for some time, through comings and goings of the gray lady at no. 27 Spitalgasse, through many patterns of light on the Alps, through alterations of the air from warm to cool to wet. The sender, a short fat man with a mustache, is insulted. He crated the chemicals at his factory in Basle as soon as he heard the awnings open over the market. He carried the boxes to the train while the clouds were still in the same positions as when the contract was signed. What more could he do?

In a world where time cannot be measured, there are no clocks, no calendars, no definite appointments. Events are triggered by other events, not by time. A house is begun when stone and lumber arrive at the building site. The stone quarry delivers stone when the quarryman needs money. The barrister leaves home to argue a case at the Supreme Court when his daughter makes a joke about his growing bald. Education at the gymnasium in Berne is concluded when the student has passed his examinations. Trains leave the station at the Bahnhofplatz when the cars are filled with passengers.

In a world where time is a quality, events are recorded by the color of the sky, the tone of the boatman's call on the Aare, the feeling of happiness or fear when a person comes into a room. The birth of a baby, the patent of an invention, the meeting of two people are not fixed points in time, held down by hours and minutes. Instead, events glide through the space of the imagination, materialized by a look, a desire. Likewise, the time between two events is long or short, depending on the background of contrasting events, the intensity of illumination, the degree of light and shadow, the view of the participants.

Some people attempt to quantify time, to parse time, to dissect time. They are turned to stone. Their bodies stand frozen on street corners, cold, hard, and heavy. In time, these statues are taken to the quarryman, who cuts them up evenly in equal sections and sells them for houses when he needs the money.

On the corner of Kramgasse and Theaterplatz there is a small outdoor café with six blue tables and a row of blue petunias in the chef's window box, and from this café one can see and hear the whole of Berne. People drift through the arcades on Kramgasse, talking and stopping to buy linen or wristwatches or cinnamon; a group of eight-year-old boys, let out for morning recess from the grammar school on Kochergasse, follow their teacher in single file through the streets to the banks of the Aare; smoke rises lazily from a mill just over the river; water gurgles from the spouts of the Zähringer Fountain; the giant clock tower on Kramgasse strikes the quarter hour.

If, for the moment, one ignores the sounds and the smells of the city, a remarkable sight will be seen. Two men at the corner of Kochergasse are trying to part but cannot, as if they would never see each other again. They say goodbye, start to walk in opposite directions, then hurry back together and embrace. Nearby, a middle-aged woman sits on the stone rim of a fountain, weeping quietly. She grips the stone with her yellow stained hands, grips it so hard that the blood rushes from her hands, and she stares in despair at the ground. Her loneliness has the permanence of a person who believes she will never see other people again. Two women in sweaters stroll down Kramgasse, arm in arm, laughing with such abandon that they could be thinking no thought of the future.

In fact, this is a world without future. In this world, time is a line that terminates at the present, both in reality and in the mind. In this world, no person can imagine the future. Imagining the future is no more possible than seeing colors beyond violet: the senses cannot conceive what may lie past the visible end of the spectrum. In a world without future, each parting of friends is a death. In a world without future, each loneliness is final. In a world without future, each laugh is the last laugh. In a world without future, beyond the present lies nothingness, and people cling to the present as if hanging from a cliff.

A person who cannot imagine the future is a person who cannot contemplate the results of his actions. Some are thus paralyzed into inaction. They lie in their beds through the day, wide awake but afraid to put on their clothes. They drink coffee and look at photographs. Others leap out of bed in the morning, unconcerned that each action leads into nothingness, unconcerned that they cannot plan out their lives. They live moment to moment, and each moment is full. Still others substitute the past for the future. They recount each memory, each action taken, each cause and effect, and are fascinated by how events have delivered them to this moment, the last moment of the world, the termination of the line that is time.

In the little café with the six outdoor tables and the row of petunias, a young man sits with his coffee and pastry. He has been idly observing the street. He has seen the two laughing women in sweaters, the middle-aged woman at the fountain, the two friends who keep repeating goodbyes. As he sits, a dark rain cloud makes its way over the city. But the young man remains at his table. He can imagine only the present, and at this moment the present is a blackening sky but no rain. As he sips the coffee and eats the pastry, he marvels at how the end of the world is so dark. Still there is no rain, and he squints at his paper in the dwindling light, trying to read the last sentence that he will read in his life. Then, rain. The young man goes inside, takes off his wet jacket, marvels at how the world ends in rain. He discusses food with the chef, but he is not waiting for the rain to stop because he is not waiting for anything. In a world without future, each moment is the end of the world. After twenty minutes, the storm cloud passes, the rain stops, and the sky brightens. The young man returns to his table, marvels that the world ends in sunlight.

• 15 June 1905

In this world, time is a visible dimension. Just as one may look off in the distance and see houses, trees, mountain peaks that are landmarks in space, so one may look out in another direction and see births, marriages, deaths that are signposts in time, stretching off dimly into the far future. And just as one may choose whether to stay in one place or run to another, so one may choose his motion along the axis of time. Some people fear traveling far from a comfortable moment. They remain close to one temporal location, barely crawling past a familiar occasion. Others gallop recklessly into the future, without preparation for the rapid sequence of passing events.

At the polytechnic in Zürich, a young man and his mentor sit in a small library, quietly discussing the young man's doctoral work. It is the month of December, and a fire blazes in the fireplace with the white marble mantel. The young man and his teacher sit in pleasant oak chairs next to a round table, strewn with pages of calculations. The research has been difficult. Each month for the past eighteen months, the young man has met his professor here in this room, asked his professor for guidance and hope, gone away to work for another month, come back with new questions. The professor has always provided answers. Again today, the professor explains. While his teacher is speaking, the young man gazes out the window, studies the way snow clings to the spruce beside the building, wonders how he will manage on his own once he has received his degree. Sitting in his chair, the young man steps hesitantly forward in time, only minutes into the future, shudders at the cold and uncertainty. He pulls back. Much better to stay in this moment, beside the warm fire, beside the warm help of his mentor. Much better to stop movement in time. And so, on this day in the small library, the young man remains. His friends pass by, look in briefly to see him stopped in this moment, continue on to the future at their own paces.

At no. 27 Viktoriastrasse, in Berne, a young woman lies on her bed. The sounds of her parents' fighting drift up to her room. She covers her ears and stares at a photograph on her table, a photograph of herself as a child, squatting at the beach with her mother and father. Against one wall of her room stands a chestnut bureau. A porcelain wash basin sits on the bureau. The blue paint on the wall is peeling and cracked. At the foot of her bed, a suitcase is open, half-filled with clothes. She stares at the photograph, then out into time. The future is beckoning. She makes up her mind. Without finishing her packing, she rushes out of her house, this point of her life, rushes straight to the future. She rushes past one year ahead, five years, ten years, twenty years, finally puts on the brakes. But she is moving so fast that she cannot slow down until she is fifty years old. Events have raced by her vision and barely been seen. A balding solicitor who got her pregnant and then left. A blur of a year at the university. A small apartment in Lausanne for some period of time. A girlfriend in Fribourg. Scattered visits to her parents gone gray. The hospital room where her mother died. The damp apartment in Zürich, smelling of garlic, where her father died. A letter from her daughter, living somewhere in England.

The woman catches her breath. She is fifty years old. She lies on her bed, tries to remember her life, stares at a photograph of herself as a child, squatting at the beach with her mother and father.

It is Tuesday morning in Berne. The thick-fingered baker on Marktgasse is shouting at a woman who has not paid her last bill, is flailing his arms while she quietly puts her new purchase of zwieback in her bag. Outside the baker's shop, a child is skating after a ball tossed from a first-floor window, the child's skates clicking on the stone street. On the east end of Marktgasse, where the street joins Kramgasse, a man and woman are standing close in the shadow of an arcade. Two men are walking past with newspapers under their arms. Three hundred meters to the south, a warbler is flying lazily over the Aare.

The world stops.

The baker's mouth halts in mid-sentence. The child floats in mid-stride, the ball hangs in the air. The man and woman become statues under the arcade. The two men become statues, their conversation stopped as if the needle of a phonograph had been lifted. The bird freezes in flight, fixed like a stage prop suspended over the river.

A microsecond later, the world starts again.

The baker continues his harangue as if nothing had happened. So, too, the child races after the ball. The man and woman press closer together. The two men continue debating the rise in the beef market. The bird flaps its wings and continues its arc over the Aare.

Minutes later, the world stops again. Then starts again. Stops. Starts.

What world is this? In this world time is not continuous. In this world time is discontinuous. Time is a stretch of nerve fibers: seemingly continuous from a distance but disjointed close up, with microscopic gaps between fibers. Nervous action flows through one segment of time, abruptly stops, pauses, leaps through a vacuum, and resumes in the neighboring segment.

So tiny are the disconnections in time that a single second would have to be magnified and dissected into one thousand parts and each of those parts into one thousand parts before a single missing part of time could be spotted. So tiny are the disconnections in time that the gaps between segments are practically imperceptible. After each restart of time, the new world looks just like the old. The positions and motions of clouds appear exactly the same, the trajectories of birds, the flow of conversations, thoughts.

The segments of time fit together almost perfectly, but not quite perfectly. On occasion, very slight displacements occur. For example, on this Tuesday in Berne, a young man and a young woman, in their late twenties, stand beneath a street lamp on Gerberngasse. They met one month ago. He loves her desperately, but he has already been crushed by a woman who left him without warning, and he is frightened of love. He must be sure with this woman. He studies her face, pleads silently for her true feelings, searches for the smallest sign, the slightest movement of her brow, the vaguest reddening of her cheeks, the moistness of her eyes.

In truth, she loves him back, but she cannot put her love in words. Instead, she smiles at him, unaware of his fear. As they stand beneath the street lamp, time stops and restarts. Afterwards, the tilt of their heads is precisely the same, the cycle of their heartbeats shows no alteration. But somewhere in the deep pools of the woman's mind, a dim thought has appeared that was not there before. The young woman reaches for this new thought, into her unconscious, and as she does so a gossamer vacancy crosses her smile. This slight hesitation would be invisible to any but the closest scrutiny, yet the urgent young man has noticed it and taken it for his sign. He tells the young woman that he cannot see her again, returns to his small apartment on Zeughausgasse, decides to move to Zürich and work in his uncle's bank. The young woman walks slowly home from the lamppost on Gerberngasse and wonders why the young man did not love her.

• INTERLUDE

Einstein and Besso sit in a small fishing boat at anchor in the river. Besso is eating a cheese sandwich while Einstein puffs on his pipe and slowly reels in a lure.

"Do you usually catch anything here, smack in the middle of the Aare?" asks Besso, who has never been fishing with Einstein before.

"Never," answers Einstein, who continues to cast.

"Maybe we should move closer to the shore, by those reeds."

"We could," says Einstein. "Never caught anything there, either. You got another sandwich in that bag?"

Besso hands Einstein a sandwich and a beer. He feels slightly guilty for asking his friend to take him along on this Sunday afternoon. Einstein was planning to go fishing alone, in order to think.

"Eat," says Besso. "You need a break from pulling in all those fish."

Einstein lowers his lure into Besso's lap and starts eating. For a while, the two friends are silent. A small red skiff passes by, making waves, and the fishing boat bobs up and down.

After lunch, Einstein and Besso remove the seats in the boat and lie on their backs, looking up at the sky. For today, Einstein has given up fishing.

"What shapes do you see in the clouds, Michele?" asks Einstein.

"I see a goat chasing a man who is frowning."

"You are a practical man, Michele." Einstein gazes at the clouds but is thinking of his project. He wants to tell Besso about his dreams, but he cannot bring himself to do it.

"I think you will succeed with your theory of time," says

Besso. "And when you do, we will go fishing and you will explain it to me. When you become famous, you'll remember that you told me first, here in this boat."

Einstein laughs, and the clouds rock back and forth with his laughter.

Emanating from a cathedral in the center of Rome, a line of ten thousand people stretches radially outward, like the hand of a giant clock, out to the edge of the city, and beyond. Yet these patient pilgrims are directed inward, not out. They are waiting their turn to enter the Temple of Time. They are waiting to bow to the Great Clock. They have traveled long distances, even from other countries, to visit this shrine. Now they stand quietly as the line creeps forward through immaculate streets. Some read from their prayer books. Some hold children. Some eat figs or drink water. And as they wait, they seem oblivious to the passage of time. They do not glance at their watches, for they do not own watches. They do not listen for chimes from a clock tower, for clock towers do not exist. Watches and clocks are forbidden, except for the Great Clock in the Temple of Time.

Inside the temple, twelve pilgrims stand in a circle around the Great Clock, one pilgrim for each hour mark on the huge configuration of metal and glass. Inside their circle, a massive bronze pendulum swings from a height of twelve meters, glints in the candlelight. The pilgrims chant with each period of the pendulum, chant with each measured increment of time. The pilgrims chant with each minute subtracted from their lives. This is their sacrifice.

After an hour by the Great Clock, the pilgrims depart and another twelve file through the tall portals. This procession continued for centuries.

Long ago, before the Great Clock, time was measured by changes in heavenly bodies: the slow sweep of stars across the night sky, the arc of the sun and variation in light, the waxing and waning of the moon, tides, seasons. Time was measured also by heartbeats, the rhythms of drowsiness and sleep, the recurrence of hunger, the menstrual cycles of women, the duration of loneliness. Then, in a small town in Italy, the first mechanical clock was built. People were spellbound. Later they were horrified. Here was a human invention that quantified the passage of time, that laid ruler and compass to the span of desire, that measured out exactly the moments of a life. It was magical, it was unbearable, it was outside natural law. Yet the clock could not be ignored. It would have to be worshipped. The inventor was persuaded to build the Great Clock. Afterwards, he was killed and all other clocks were destroyed. Then the pilgrimages began.

In some ways, life goes on the same as before the Great Clock. The streets and alleyways of towns sparkle with the laughter of children. Families gather in good times to eat smoked beef and drink beer. Boys and girls glance shyly at each other across the atrium of an arcade. Painters adorn houses and buildings with their paintings. Philosophers contemplate. But every breath, every crossing of legs, every romantic desire has a slight gnarliness that gets caught in the mind. Every action, no matter how little, is no longer free. For all people know that in a certain cathedral in the center of Rome swings a massive bronze pendulum exquisitely connected to ratchets and gears, swings a massive bronze pendulum that measures out their lives. And each person knows that at some time he must confront the loose intervals of his life, must pay homage to the Great Clock. Each man and woman must journey to the Temple of Time.

Thus, on any day, at any hour of any day, a line of ten thousand stretches radially outward from the center of Rome, a line of pilgrims waiting to bow to the Great Clock. They stand quietly, reading prayer books, holding their children. They stand quietly, but secretly they seethe with their anger. For they must watch measured that which should not be measured. They must watch the precise passage of minutes and decades. They have been trapped by their own inventiveness and audacity. And they must pay with their lives.

· 20 June 1905

In this world, time is a local phenomenon. Two clocks close together tick at nearly the same rate. But clocks separated by distance tick at different rates, the farther apart the more out of step. What holds true for clocks holds true also for the rate of heartbeats, the pace of inhales and exhales, the movement of wind in tall grass. In this world, time flows at different speeds in different locations.

Since commerce requires a temporal union, commerce between cities does not exist. The separations between cities are too great. For if the time needed to count a thousand Swiss franc notes is ten minutes in Berne and one hour in Zürich, how can the two cities do business together? In consequence, each city is alone. Each city is an island. Each city must grow its own plums and its cherries, each city must raise its own cattle and pigs, each city must build its own mills. Each city must live on its own.

On occasion, a traveler will venture from one city to another. Is he perplexed? What took seconds in Berne might take hours in Fribourg, or days in Lucerne. In the time for a leaf to fall in one place, a flower could bloom in another. In the duration of a thunderclap in one place, two people could fall in love in another. In the time that a boy grows into a man, a drop of rain might slide down a windowpane. Yet the traveler is unaware of these discrepancies. As he moves from one timescape to the next, the traveler's body adjusts to the local movement of time. If every heartbeat, every swing of a pendulum, every unfolding of wings of a cormorant are all harmonized together, how could a traveler know that he has passed to a new zone of time? If the pace of human desires stays proportionally the same with the motion of waves on a pond, how could the traveler know that something has changed?

Only when the traveler communicates with the city of departure does he realize he has entered a new domain of time. Then he learns that while he has been gone his clothing shop has wildly prospered and diversified, or his daughter has lived her life and grown old, or perhaps his neighbor's wife has just completed the song she was singing when he left his front gate. It is then the traveler learns that he is cut off in time, as well as in space. No traveler goes back to his city of origin.

Some people delight in isolation. They argue that their city is the grandest of cities, so why would they want communion with other cities. What silk could be softer than the silk from their own factories? What cows could be stronger than the cows in their own pastures? What watches could be finer than the watches in their own shops? Such people stand on their balconies at morning, as the sun rises over the mountains, and never look past the outskirts of town.

Others want contact. They endlessly question the rare traveler who wanders into their city, ask him about places he has been, ask him about the color of other sunsets, the height of people and animals, the languages spoken, the customs of courtship, inventions. In time, one of the curious sets out to see for himself, leaves his city to explore other cities, becomes a traveler. He never returns.

This world of the locality of time, this world of isolation yields a rich variety of life. For without the blending of cities, life can develop in a thousand different ways. In one city, people may live together closely, in another far apart. In one city, people may dress modestly, in another they may wear no clothes at all. In one city, people may mourn the death of enemies, in another they may have neither enemies nor friends. In one city, people may walk, in another they may ride in vehicles of strange invention. Such variety and more exists in regions only one hundred kilometers apart. Just beyond a mountain, just beyond a river lies a different life. Yet these lives do not speak to each other. These lives do not share. These lives do not nurture each other. The abundances caused by isolation are stifled by the same isolation.

It is graduation day at Agassiz Gymnasium. One hundred twenty-nine boys in white shirts and brown ties stand on marble steps and fidget in the sun while the headmaster reads out their names. On the front lawn, parents and relatives listen halfheartedly, stare at the ground, doze in their chairs. The valedictorian delivers his address in a monotone. He smiles weakly when handed his medal and drops it in a bush after the ceremony. No one congratulates him. The boys, their mothers, fathers, sisters walk listlessly to houses on Amthausgasse and

Aarstrasse, or to the waiting benches near the Bahnhofplatz, sit after the noon meal, play cards to pass time, nap. Dress clothes are folded and put away for another occasion. At the end of the summer, some of the boys go to university in Berne or in Zürich, some work in their fathers' businesses, some travel to Germany or France in search of a job. These passages take place indifferently, mechanically, like the back-and-forth swing of a pendulum, like a chess game in which each move is forced. For in this world, the future is fixed.

This is a world in which time is not fluid, parting to make way for events. Instead, time is a rigid, bonelike structure, extending infinitely ahead and behind, fossilizing the future as well as the past. Every action, every thought, every breath of wind, every flight of birds is completely determined, forever.

In the performing hall of the Stadttheater, a ballerina moves across the stage and takes to the air. She hangs for a moment and then alights on the floor. *Saut, batterie, saut.* Legs cross and flutter, arms unfold into an open arch. Now she prepares for a *pirouette*, right leg moving back to fourth position, pushing off on one foot, arms coming in to speed the turn. She is precision. She is a clock. In her mind, while she dances, she thinks she should have floated a little on one leap, but she cannot float because her movements are not hers. Every interaction of her body with floor or with space is predetermined to a billionth of an inch. There is no room to float. To float would indicate a slight uncertainty, while there is no uncertainty. And so she moves around the stage with clocklike inevitability, makes no unexpected leaps or dares, touches down precisely on the chalk, does not dream of unplanned *cabrioles*.

In a world of fixed future, life is an infinite corridor of rooms, one room lit at each moment, the next room dark but prepared. We walk from room to room, look into the room that is lit, the present moment, then walk on. We do not know the rooms ahead, but we know we cannot change them. We are spectators of our lives.

The chemist who works at the pharmaceutical on Kochergasse walks through the town on his afternoon break. He stops at the shop selling clocks on Marktgasse, buys a sandwich at the bakery next door, continues toward the woods and the river. He owes his friend money but prefers to buy himself presents. As he walks, admiring his new coat, he decides he can pay his friend back the next year, or perhaps never at all. And who can blame him? In a world of fixed future, there can be no right or wrong. Right and wrong demand freedom of choice, but if each action is already chosen, there can be no freedom of choice. In a world of fixed future, no person is responsible. The rooms are already arranged. The chemist thinks all these thoughts as he steps along the path through the Brunngasshalde and breathes the moist air of the forest. He almost permits himself a smile, so pleased is he at his decision. He breathes the moist air and feels oddly free to do as he pleases, free in a world without freedom.

• 25 JUNE 1905

Sunday afternoon. People stroll down Aarstrasse, wearing Sunday clothes and full of Sunday dinner, speaking softly beside the murmur of the river. The shops are closed. Three women walk down Marktgasse, stop to read advertisements, stop to peer in windows, walk on quietly. An innkeeper scrubs his steps, sits and reads a paper, leans against the sandstone wall and shuts his eyes. The streets are sleeping. The streets are sleeping, and through the air there floats music from a violin.

In the middle of a room with books on tables, a young man

stands and plays his violin. He loves his violin. He makes a gentle melody. And as he plays, he looks out to the street below, notices a couple close together, looks at them with deep brown eyes, and looks away. He stands so still. His music is the only movement, his music fills the room. He stands so still and thinks about his wife and infant son, who occupy the room downstairs.

And as he plays, another man, identical, stands in the middle of a room and plays his violin. The other man looks to the street below, notices a couple close together, looks away, and thinks about his wife and son. And as he plays, a third man stands and plays his violin. Indeed, there are a fourth and fifth, there is a countless number of young men standing in their rooms and playing violins. There is an infinite number of melodies and thoughts. And this one hour, while the young men play their violins, is not one hour but many hours. For time is like the light between two mirrors. Time bounces back and forth, producing an infinite number of images, of melodies, of thoughts. It is a world of countless copies.

As he thinks, the first man feels the others. He feels their music and their thoughts. He feels himself repeated a thousand times, feels this room with books repeated a thousand times.

He feels his thoughts repeated. Should he leave his wife? What about that moment in the library of the polytechnic when she looked at him across the desk? What about her thick brown hair? But what comfort has she given him? What solitude, besides this hour to play his violin?

He feels the others. He feels himself repeated a thousand times, feels this room repeated a thousand times, feels his thoughts repeated. Which repetition is his own, his true identity, his future self? Should he leave his wife? What about that moment in the library of the polytechnic? What comfort has she given him? What solitude, besides this hour to play his violin? His thoughts bounce back and forth a thousand times between each copy of himself, grow weaker with each bounce. Should he leave his wife? What comfort has she given him? What solitude? His thoughts grow dimmer with each reflection. What comfort has she given him? What solitude? His thoughts grow dimmer until he hardly remembers what the questions were, or why. What solitude? He looks out to the empty street and plays. His music floats and fills the room, and when the hour passes that was countless hours, he remembers only music.

Every Tuesday, a middle-aged man brings stones from the quarry east of Berne to the masonry on Hodlerstrasse. He has a wife, two children grown and gone, a tubercular brother who lives in Berlin. He wears a gray wool coat in all seasons, works in the quarry until after dark, has dinner with his wife and goes to bed, tends his garden on Sundays. And on Tuesday mornings, he loads his truck with stones and comes to town.

When he comes, he stops on Marktgasse to purchase flour and sugar. He spends a half hour sitting quietly in the back pew of St. Vincent's. He stops at the Post Bureau to send a letter to Berlin. And as he passes people on the street, his eyes are on the ground. Some people know him, try to catch his eye or say hello. He mumbles and walks on. Even when he delivers his stones to Hodlerstrasse, he cannot look the mason in the eye. Instead, he looks aside, he talks to the wall in answer to the mason's friendly chatter, he stands in a corner while his stones are weighed.

Forty years ago in school, one afternoon in March, he urinated in class. He could not hold it in. Afterwards, he tried to stay in his chair, but the other boys saw the puddle and made him walk around the room, round and round. They pointed at the wet spot on his pants and howled. That day the sunlight looked like streams of milk as it poured whitely through the windows and spilled onto the floorboards of the room. Two dozen jackets hung from hooks beside the door. Chalk marks stretched across the blackboard, the names of Europe's capitals. The desks had swivel tops and drawers. His had "Johann" carved in the upper right. The air was moist and close from the steam pipes. A clock with big red hands read 2:15. And the boys hooted at him, hooted at him as they chased him around the room, with the wet spot on his pants. They hooted and called him "bladder baby, bladder baby, bladder baby."

That memory has become his life. When he wakes up in the morning, he is the boy who urinated in his pants. When he passes people on the street, he knows they see the wet spot on his pants. He glances at his pants and looks away. When his children visit, he stays within his room and talks to them through the door. He is the boy who could not hold it in.

But what is the past? Could it be, the firmness of the past is just illusion? Could the past be a kaleidoscope, a pattern of images that shift with each disturbance of a sudden breeze, a laugh, a thought? And if the shift is everywhere, how would we know?

In a world of shifting past, one morning the quarryman awakes and is no more the boy who could not hold it in. That afternoon in March long gone was just another afternoon. On that afternoon forgotten, he sat in class, recited when the teacher called him, went skating with the other boys after school. Now he owns a quarry. He has nine suits of clothes. He buys fine pottery for his wife and takes long walks with her on Sunday afternoons. He visits friends on Amthausgasse and Aarstrasse, smiles at them and shakes their hand. He sponsors concerts at the Casino.

One morning he wakes up and . . .

As the sun rises over the city, ten thousand people yawn and take their toast and coffee. Ten thousand fill the arcades of Kramgasse or go to work on Speichergasse or take their children to the park. Each has memories: a father who could not love his child, a brother who always won, a lover with a delicious kiss, a moment of cheating on a school examination, the stillness spreading from a fresh snowfall, the publication of a poem. In a world of shifting past, these memories are wheat in wind, fleeting dreams, shapes in clouds. Events, once happened, lose reality, alter with a glance, a storm, a night. In time, the past never happened. But who could know? Who could know that the past is not as solid as this instant, when the sun streams over the Bernese Alps and the shopkeepers sing as they raise their awnings and the quarryman begins to load his truck.

"Stop eating so much," says the grandmother, tapping her son on the shoulder. "You'll die before me and who will take care of my silver." The family is having a picnic on the bank of the Aare, ten kilometers south of Berne. The girls have finished their lunch and chase each other around a spruce tree. Finally dizzy, they collapse in the thick grass, lie still for a moment, then roll on the ground and get dizzy again. The son and his very fat wife and the grandmother sit on a blanket, eating smoked ham, cheese, sourdough bread with mustard, grapes, chocolate cake. As they eat and drink, a gentle breeze comes over the river and they breathe in the sweet summer air. The son takes off his shoes and wiggles his toes in the grass.

Suddenly a flock of birds darts overhead. The young man leaps from the blanket and runs after them, without taking time to put on his shoes. He disappears over the hill. Soon he is joined by others, who have spotted the birds from the city.

One bird has alighted in a tree. A woman climbs the trunk, reaches out to catch the bird, but the bird jumps quickly to a higher branch. She climbs farther up, cautiously straddles a branch and creeps outward. The bird hops back to the lower branch. As the woman hangs helplessly up in the tree, another bird has touched down to eat seeds. Two men sneak up behind it, carrying a giant bell jar. But the bird is too fast for them and takes to the air, merging again with the flock.

Now the birds fly through the town. The pastor at St. Vincent's Cathedral stands in the belfry, tries to coax the birds into the arched window. An old woman in the Kleine Schanze gardens sees the birds momentarily roost in a bush. She walks slowly toward them with a bell jar, knows she has no chance of entrapping a bird, drops her jar to the ground and begins weeping.

And she is not alone in her frustration. Indeed, each man and each woman desires a bird. Because this flock of nightingales is time. Time flutters and fidgets and hops with these birds. Trap one of these nightingales beneath a bell jar and time stops. The moment is frozen for all people and trees and soil caught within.

In truth, these birds are rarely caught. The children, who alone have the speed to catch birds, have no desire to stop time. For the children, time moves too slowly already. They rush from moment to moment, anxious for birthdays and new years, barely able to wait for the rest of their lives. The elderly desperately wish to halt time, but are much too slow and fatigued to entrap any bird. For the elderly, time darts by much too quickly. They yearn to capture a single minute at the breakfast table drinking tea, or a moment when a grandchild is stuck getting out of her costume, or an afternoon when the winter sun reflects off the snow and floods the music room with light. But they are too slow. They must watch time jump and fly beyond reach.

On those occasions when a nightingale is caught, the catchers delight in the moment now frozen. They savor the precise placement of family and friends, the facial expressions, the trapped happiness over a prize or a birth or romance, the captured smell of cinnamon or white double violets. The catchers delight in the moment so frozen but soon discover that the nightingale expires, its clear, flutelike song diminishes to silence, the trapped moment grows withered and without life.

• Epilogue

A clock tower strikes eight times in the distance. The young patent clerk lifts his head from his desk, stands up and stretches, walks to the window.

Outside, the town is awake. A woman and her husband argue as she hands him his lunch. A group of boys on their way to the gymnasium on Zeughausgasse throw a soccer ball back and forth and talk excitedly about the summer vacation. Two women walk briskly toward Marktgasse carrying empty shopping sacks.

Shortly, a senior patent officer comes in the door, goes to his desk and begins working, without saying a word. Einstein turns around and looks at the clock in the corner. Three minutes after eight. He fidgets with coins in his pocket.

At four minutes past eight, the typist walks in. She sees Einstein across the room holding his handwritten manuscript and she smiles. She has already typed several of his personal papers for him in her spare time, and he always gladly pays what she asks. He is quiet, though he sometimes tells jokes. She likes him.

Einstein gives her his manuscript, his theory of time. It is six minutes past eight. He walks to his desk, glances at the stack of files, goes over to a bookshelf, and starts to remove one of the notebooks. He turns and walks back to the window. The air is unusually clear for late June. Above an apartment building, he can see the tips of the Alps, which are blue with white tops. Higher up, the tiny black speck of a bird makes slow loops in the sky.

Einstein walks back to his desk, sits down for a moment, and then returns to the window. He feels empty. He has no interest in reviewing patents or talking to Besso or thinking of physics. He feels empty, and he stares without interest at the tiny black speck and the Alps.